Animals
Don't have Ghosts

SIOBHÁN PARKINSON

Illustrated by Catherine Henderson

THE O'BRIEN PRESS
DUBLIN

First published 2002 by The O'Brien Press Ltd,
20 Victoria Road, Dublin 6, Ireland.
Tel: +353 1 4923333; Fax: +353 1 4922777
E-mail: books@obrien.ie
Website: www.obrien.ie
Reprinted 2004.

ISBN 0-86278-756-4

British Library Cataloguing-in-Publication Data.
Parkinson, Siobhán
Animals don't have ghosts.
1.Dublin (Ireland) - Social life and customs - 20th century -
Juvenile fiction 2.Children's stories
I.Title II.Henderson, Cathy
823.9'14[J]

1 2 3 4 5 6 7 8 9 10
04 05 06 07 08 09 10

The O'Brien Press receives
assistance from

the arts council
schomhairle
ealaíon

Editing, typesetting, layout, design: The O'Brien Press Ltd
Printing: Cox & Wyman Ltd

To all the country cousins,
and with special thanks once again to
Clodagh, Sarah and Darragh.

CONTENTS

1. On The Bus **page 9**

2. The Magnificent Megaloceros **17**

3. Sticky Buns and Naked People **25**

4. The Midnight Feast **41**

5. Little Boy Lost **53**

6. Dara and the Red Balloons **69**

1

On the Bus

My name's Michelle and I'm a Dub. That means I'm from Dublin. Dublin is the capital of Ireland, and it's the best and everyone else is a culchie.

My cousins Sinéad and Dara came to stay last week. They're culchies because they're from the country. They live on a farm in a place nobody ever heard of with loads of sheep and they have a cow farm next door to them.

They're not too bad, for culchies, though Dara is a bit of a baby, not even six yet, so you

can't really expect him to understand things.
Sinéad is my friend, eight like me, only sometimes she can be a bit of a goody-goody.

Uncle Dan came as well, to mind Sinéad and
Dara on the train. He's a culchie too, but
older. I like him.

When they were here, my ma
took us to see the animals in the
Natural History Museum.
That's in
town, near

the Dáil, where the government lives. We have important things in Dublin, like the Natural History Museum and the other museum with all the goldy things in it and Trinity College and the Book of Kells and the Dáil and stuff, because it's the capital, which means it is the most important place.

Dara was a bit worried about the Natural History Museum.

'I'm too young for history,' he said. 'You don't do that until first class.'

'It's not *that* sort of history,' I said.

He's a bit of an eejit, Dara.

'Natural history means animals, mostly,' Ma said.

We went on the bus. I had to explain to Sinéad and Dara about queuing. Sinéad said they knew what a queue was, but I knew she was only bluffing because there aren't any bus stops in the country. We were waiting for ages for the bus, and I asked Sinéad and Dara if they knew about banana buses. Sinéad tried to bluff on that one, too, but she made a mess of it. 'They're yellow ones,' she said.

'No, they're not. All Dublin buses are banana buses because they come in bunches!' I said.

'What?' said Sinéad. She didn't get it.

'Well, you wait and you wait and you get cold and annoyed and you're late for where you were going to and then a bus comes, and another one comes too, and a third one. They all come together, in a bunch. So we call them the banana buses. Get it? Bananas, bunches. See?'

'That's stupid,' said Sinéad.

'Why?' I asked.

'Because if they came one at a time it would be better.'

'Well, of *course* it would be better,' I said.

'That's the whole *point*. That's the joke.'

She still didn't get it. For such a clever clogs, she can be a bit dim sometimes.

The bus came in the end. It was a double-decker, which they don't have in the country, and Dara was delighted. So just for him we all went upstairs and sat on the top deck and looked down at all the people.

'Oh, look,' said Dara, 'umbrellas with legs.'

It had started to rain and people out on the

street had put up their umbrellas and, right enough, from the top of the bus they did look like umbrellas with legs.

'And look, you can see the top of the street lights,' said Sinéad. 'It's weird being up so high. I like it when the branches of the trees brush along the roof of the bus. It sounds like a rainstorm.'

'I'm on the bus,' said a voice behind us suddenly.

Dara looked around and said, 'We're *all* on the bus.'

The people sitting near us laughed, because the person wasn't talking to us.

He was talking into his mobile phone. He glared at Dara. You could see that Dara's not used to Dublin buses. Everyone is always shouting 'I'm on the bus' into their mobiles.

2

The Magnificent
Megaloceros

It was still raining when we got off the bus.

'We have gutters for the rain, see?' I said to Sinéad. 'So we don't have to go around up to our knees in muck, like in the country.'

'Hmm,' she said, 'only problem is they're full of litter.'

There were a couple of crisp bags in the gutter and one or two tissues. You couldn't really call it 'full of litter'. Sinéad exaggerates.

'Well, at least there's no cow-pats,' I said.

'Is the Natural History Museum like a zoo?' Sinéad asked. She changes the subject when she doesn't like what you say to her.

'No,' said Ma, struggling with her umbrella, 'it's not like a zoo. All the animals are dead.'

'*Dead*!' shouted Dara and Sinéad together, and they opened their eyes up very wide. I thought their eyeballs were going to pop out and roll off along the gutter.

'Loads of skeletons!' I said.

'Ooh!' they said. 'We don't like skeletons.'

For kids who go stomping around in cow pooh all the time in their wellingtons, they can be pretty squeamish.

'Well, I do!' I said.

'Are there dinosaurs?' asked Dara, hopefully,

as we went in the door.

'How could there be dinosaurs?' I said. 'Dinosaurs are extinct.'

'There could be *dead* dinosaurs,' argued Dara. 'Or dinosaur skeletons.'

'Well, there aren't,' I said.

'Are you *sure* they're dead?' asked Dara when he saw all the animals in their glass cases. He stood well back, because you never know, do you?

'Yep,' I said.

'Only they *look* real,' he said.

'Real,' I said, 'but de-e-e-a-ad,' and I put on a quivery, spooky voice and made a snatching movement to scare Dara.

He gave a little yelp, and Sinéad grabbed his hand. I think that made him feel a bit braver.

'I don't like the smell,' he said, wrinkling his nose.

'Neither do I,' said Sinéad.

'It's just the chemicals they use to keep the bodies from *rotting*,' I said cheerfully.

Dara gave another little yelp.

'But they're standing *up*,' he squeaked.

'Even so,' I said. 'They put them standing up to make them look alive, but they're dead all right.'

The amazing thing about the Natural History Museum is how *un*dead the animals look. There was a dotey little squirrel sitting there as large as life in a glass case eating a nut. Well, not really eating it. Holding it. But she looked as if she might be about to eat it, if she wasn't dead, that is.

'I thought you said there were skeletons,' Dara said.

'Look out!' I said. 'There's one behind you!'

Dara turned around with another yelp, and sure enough, there was a big, huge, ginormous animal skeleton with massive big antlery things.

'That is the biggest, hugest, most ginormous skeleton I ever saw!' Dara said, staring up at it, and he did that poppy thing with his eyeballs again.

'I bet its *ghost* is somewhere about,' I said, putting on a quivery voice and looking over my shoulder.

'Animals don't have ghosts,' said Dara, but he had a good look around him all the same, just to be sure. 'Do they?' he added a bit doubtfully.

'Hah!' I said.

'Is it a dinosaur?' Sinéad asked.

'Not exactly,' said Ma, taking off her glasses to read the little label. (I never understand why grown-ups do that. It always seems daft to me to take *off* your glasses to see something.) 'It's a "*Megaloceros giganteus*".'

'A mega-*what*-erus?' said Dara.

'Mega-loc-e-ros,' said Sinéad. She was reading the label, too. '*Megaloceros gi-gant-e-us*.'

'Wow!' said Dara. 'It *sounds* like a dinosaur.'

'It says here it's really a giant Irish deer,' said Sinéad. '"Megaloceros" is just its posh name. Isn't it magnificent!'

'Yeah,' I said. 'It's mega, all right.'

I felt sort of proud, at that moment, being a Dub and us having this great museum with this great megaloceros in it. Sinéad was right, it's true. They are. Megaloceroses, I mean; they *are* magnificent. Better than old sheep any day.

Megaloceroses definitely are magnificent, and Dublin definitely is mega.

3

Sticky Buns and
Naked People

After that we went for a little walk in St Stephen's Green, for some fresh air. It had stopped raining while we were in the museum.

That's the way I like my grass, the way they have it in St Stephen's Green, properly mown and with flower beds in the middle and nice, comfortable places to sit down and rest yourself.

'Isn't this better than the country?' I said to Sinéad. 'Nice and leafy, but no wild animals and the bus stop is only around the corner.'

I didn't see how she could possibly disagree with me. Any sane person can see that St Stephen's Green is the nicest place in the world to go for a walk. I love it, and there's always loads of people in it too, which makes it nice and friendly.

'Well, it's nice,' she said, 'but it's not the same.'

'Of course it's not the same,' I said. 'That's the whole *point*.'

'And there are raggy people drinking out of bottles over there,' she went on. 'They scare me.'

'They're only winos,' I said. 'They look scary when you're not used to them, but they're harmless. They're just poor old fellows with nowhere to go. Anyway, wait until you see the

playground, come on, it's mega.'

Even Sinéad had to admit that the playground was cool. In fact, it is pretty deadly, with not just slides and swings but things to hang out of and little tunnels to wriggle through and everything. Dara loved it too, even though he got wedged in a wriggle-tunnel because he forgot to take off his rucksack before he went in, and we had to poke him out with a stick.

Ma had brought along a bag of stale bread to feed the ducks, so after we had rescued Dara,

we headed off to the pond.

'Are you sure that's good for ducks?' asked Sinéad. 'Sliced pan, I mean.'

'Gosh, I'm sorry, we haven't got any wholemeal with bran,' I said. 'Are you worried about their little digestive systems?'

'Well, they don't eat anything like that in

the wild, do they?' said Sinéad. She knows all about that sort of thing. She's always reading encyclopaedias and watching the Discovery Channel on TV.

'No,' said Dara. 'They eat frogs and worms.'

'These are *Dublin* ducks,' I explained. 'They've been eating sliced pan for generations, and they're still alive.'

'I suppose so,' said Sinéad, though she didn't look too sure.

'Next time, we'll make a few worm sandwiches,' I said. 'They'd like those.'

Dara thought this was a great idea.

'And some frog stew,' he said, laughing his head off.

'Caterpillar salad,' said Sinéad, joining in.

'Pondweed pie,' I said.

'Frogspawn and custard,' said Sinéad.

'You're making me feel sick,' said Ma. 'Come on, let's go and eat some proper food.'

'Tadpole trifle,' Sinéad said as we left the Green.

'Megaloceros ice-cream,' hissed Dara.

Sinéad and I laughed politely, though that last suggestion didn't really make much sense.

'He's only small,' Sinéad whispered to me.

Grafton Street was really buzzing. There were people with a megaphone talking about God and singing hymns, and there were people with buckets collecting money for charity, and there were those little horse-drawn carriages lined up waiting for passengers, and there was somebody making sausage dogs out of pink balloons, and somebody else pretending to be a statue, all silvery, even his face, and there were people with fiddles and things playing tunes. And there were millions and millions of people, big ones and little ones, with their shopping and their buggies, and everyone was talking nineteen to the dozen and hurrying along, except the people who had stopped for a few minutes to text their friends or when they met someone they knew.

'Isn't this *great*?' I said to Sinéad.

'Um,' she said. That's what she always says when she's gobsmacked but doesn't want to let on.

We went to Bewley's then and we got a table under the special windows with all the butterflies on them and we had sticky buns and big glasses of milk.

'I like this place,' said Dara. 'Only there's too many people.'

'No there aren't,' I said. 'There's just the

right amount of people. It's more interesting when there are lots of people to look at.'

'That family at the next table,' said Dara, 'the ones with the lovely baby, I think maybe they are from India or somewhere like that. They have a different language. Are they on their holidays?'

'No, I think they probably live here,' said my ma. 'Lots of people are coming to Dublin to live now, from all sorts of countries. China, Nigeria, Bosnia, Spain, everywhere. And, of course, they all speak different languages. It's very exciting.'

'There's only Irish people in Inishbeg,' said Dara.

That's where they live. It's the smallest place in the world. It's only got their house in it. It's not even on the map. Sinéad says that's because the map people forgot, but I know it's because it's so tiny.

'Boring,' I said.

'It's not boring,' said Sinéad. She always sticks up for the country. Well, you can't blame her, that's where she's from.

Still, it's perfectly obvious that having people from all over the world is much more interesting than just Irish people, so really I couldn't be bothered arguing about it.

'Now, children,' said Ma, getting ready to go.

I don't like that 'now, children' thing she says. It usually means there is going to be something educational or with lots of vitamins coming up. I didn't think it was going to be vitamins because we'd already eaten.

'Ah no, Ma,' I said. 'We've had enough culture for one day.'

'What?' said Ma, putting on this shocked voice. 'Do you mean to say that you're not interested in showing your cousins our beautiful National Gallery?'

'That's right, Ma,' I said. 'Not interested. Not a bit.'

'But Michelle, these children have no art galleries where they come from, have you Sinéad?'

'Um,' said Sinéad. I could see she didn't want to admit to not having any art galleries in Inishbeg.

The National Gallery was all right really. I

like it if only we don't stay too long. The best room is the one with the two big sweepy staircases like out of *Beauty and the Beast*. Sinéad and I played princesses for a bit, gliding down the stairs, holding our ballgowns up so we wouldn't trip over them.

Dara was looking at this picture of two men fighting, Cain and Abel, and they were naked. Pictures of naked people always make me cold, so I usually don't look.

'Were Cain and Abel a very long time ago?' Dara asked.

'Oh yes,' I said. 'It's in the Bible, so it must be ages ago.' I was quite proud of knowing that. People think I don't listen in class, but I do if it's interesting.

'That's what I thought,' he said, 'because it must have been before they invented clothes.' I never thought of that before. Old Dara's not as goofy as he looks.

Ma said we all had to choose a favourite picture. Sinéad whispered to me that was just a way of getting us to look at the pictures, but we did it anyway, to please Ma. After all, she'd bought us the buns and all, so fair's fair.

I liked the one of the fellow in all the pink clothes and the cape and everything with the bows on his shoes and I was trying to get Sinéad to come and look at it, but she wanted me to look at her favourite. It was the girl with the geese and all the blue flowers. (I knew she'd choose a country one.) She pulled me over to it and she was all excited and pointing at it and talking about how she liked the flowers and everything, and she stuck her finger out to show me something.

'Don't **TOUCH!**' yelled a voice, and this great, big, cross woman in a uniform came belting across the room, shaking her fist and

shouting at Sinéad. 'That's a very valuable painting. Do you want to go to jail?'

Poor old Sinéad was quivering. 'Jail?' she whispered. 'No!' Her voice was really tiny.

'She didn't mean any harm,' I said, looking around desperately for my ma, but she was nowhere to be seen. Typical of grown-ups. Never there when you need them. 'She's only up from the country. She doesn't know the rules. She didn't mean it.'

'The country?' said the woman, calming down a bit. 'Ah well, so. Country children are usually well-behaved. Look, we won't put you in jail this time. But be more careful. Stand well back from the paintings, OK?'

I didn't like that bit about country children being so great, but I was glad she wasn't going to put Sinéad in jail. You'd miss her, even if she is a bit of a goody-goody.

'Yes, teacher,' said Sinéad.

'I'm not a teacher,' said the woman, laughing now. 'But maybe I sounded like one, did I?'

'No,' said Sinéad. 'My teacher is nice.'

That made the woman laugh even more.

We went looking for Ma then, and we found her looking at the picture Dara liked, which was the colouredy racehorse. We couldn't see that it was a horse, the picture was so swirly, but when he pointed it out, sure enough, it was.

After we'd all chosen a favourite picture, Ma said it was time to go home because Uncle Dan and Nana would be wondering where we were, so we went home for our tea.

4

The Midnight Feast

We live in a nice, cosy house with next-door neighbours, not like in the country where the houses are stuck out in the middle of the fields.

'It's a very *small* house,' Dara kept saying.

'So are *you*,' I said. 'You're very small.'

That stumped him.

It *is* on the small side, I suppose, our house. Three visitors was a bit of a squeeze, along with me and my ma and my nana. You nearly had to make an appointment to go to the toilet.

'We have two bathrooms at home,' Dara said, and he was dancing up and down because he needed to go.

'Well, you must be very dirty if you need two bathrooms,' I said.

It's true, there's an awful lot of muck in the country – it's no wonder they need two bathrooms.

Anyway, we haven't got enough bedrooms for so many people, so Dara had the sofa bed in the sitting room, and Uncle Dan slept in the kitchen on a camp bed that we borrowed from next door.

Uncle Dan said he had to go out on a bit of business after tea. He said he wouldn't be too late home, but he still wasn't home by the time we went to bed.

I waited a while, until I was sure everyone was asleep.

Then I crept out of bed and tiptoed downstairs. I creaked open the sitting-room door just a crack. I could see Dara, all curled up like a prawn on the sofa bed.

'RRRarrr!' I roared softly. 'RRRRarrrr!'

Dara sprang up in the sofa bed and looked around him. I could see him by the street light that's outside the sitting-room window. He was still half-asleep, so he didn't notice that the door was slightly open.

'RRRarrr!' I went again.

'Who's there?' yelped Dara. 'Who is it? Uncle Dan? Uncle Dan!'

'Sssssnot Ooooncle Daaaaan,' I crooned

through the crack in the door.

'Who is it then?' Dara was searching everywhere for where the voice was coming from,
but I stood well back behind the door so he
couldn't see me.

'Ssssme! Ssssmegalocccerross!' I purred.
'Ssssmegaloceros the MaaaaagNIFicent!
RRRarrr!'

'Meg-, Mega-, Megaloceros the Mag-, Mag-,
Magnificent?' squeaked Dara. 'But you're
dead.'

'Preee-ccciisely,' I hissed. 'Ha-ha-ha-ha!'
And I rattled the umbrellas in the umbrella
stand in the hall to make a skeleton sound.

'Wh-, wh-, whatcha want?' asked Dara.

'Ducks!' I said.

'What?'

'Ducks. Nice, big, fat ducks. I want ducks.
I'm tired of roaming around Stephen's Green
at night and eating those stringy city ducks

full of sliced pan. I want some nice, juicy country ducks with frogs and worms in them. Do you know where I could get some?'

'N-n-no!' said Dara.

'Are you shhhhhuuuure?' I asked.

'Yeah. I'm sure.'

'Because if I can't get nice country ducks,' I went on, 'I'll have to eat country CHILDREN!' And I burst out laughing and opened the door wide so he could see it was only me.

'Waaaaah! Waaah! Waaah!' went Dara. 'Waaah! Waaah! Waaah!' He couldn't stop. He was hysterical. 'Waaaaah!' He's such a baby.

I ran into the room and jumped on the

bed beside him.

'Stop, stop, stop!' I kept whispering loudly. 'Stop! It's only me, Dara. I was only pulling your leg! You didn't really think I was a megaloceros ghost, did you? Animals don't have ghosts.'

'Wah! Wah!' Dara's mouth was opening and closing, and there were tears everywhere and his face was bright red and he was rocking back and forth.

'There, there,' I said, and I put my arms around him and hugged him. 'There, there. I'm sorry, I'm sorry, I didn't mean to frighten you.'

'You did,' he sobbed.

'Yeah, you're right, I did,' I said. 'But I only meant to frighten you a little bit. I didn't think you'd be this upset. I'm sorry.' I really was sorry. Dara's OK.

I was terrified that Uncle Dan was going to

come in from the pub at any minute and want to know what was going on.

'I'll tell you what,' I said, 'you little eejit. Let's go into the kitchen and make some drinking chocolate.'

'Are we allowed?' he asked, in between sobs.

'No,' I said. 'But that makes it more fun.'

He laughed then. I was glad to see a laugh on his face. I thought he was going to spend all night crying and wake up all the grown-ups, and then I'd be in right trouble.

So Dara put on his dressing gown, and we shuffled off into the kitchen, and we boiled up a big saucepan of milk. I didn't have a dressing gown handy, so I put Uncle Dan's

duvet around me.

'Tell you what,' I whispered, 'you mind the milk, and I'll go and wake Sinéad, and we'll have a little midnight feast. Would you like that?'

He said he would, so I creaked upstairs and got Sinéad. She was still half-asleep by the time I got her down to the kitchen. I think if she'd been properly awake she'd have said no, but now that she was there, it was too late to go back to bed.

There was a bit of almond ring left that Ma had bought in Bewley's, and we dipped it into our drinking chocolate, and it was gorgeous, all soft and sloppy and chocolatey.

Then we heard Uncle Dan's key in the lock and we threw all the cups in the sink and raced back to bed.

I'd just got as far as my own bed when I realised I was still all wrapped up in Uncle Dan's duvet.

'What'll I do about Uncle Dan's duvet?' I asked Sinéad, giggling.

'You'd better take it down to him,' she said. 'Otherwise he'll freeze.'

So I went downstairs and knocked on the kitchen door.

Uncle Dan opened the door, in his pyjamas already.

'I thought you might need this,' I said, and I stuffed the duvet at him.

He didn't think it was a bit strange that I had his duvet. At any rate, he didn't ask any questions.

'Musha, thanks,' he said, in his country voice.

'Musha, good night,' I said, and we both laughed.

Next morning, Nana wanted to know where all the cups had come from, and she complained that somebody had left a dirty saucepan in the sink, and how the milk was stuck to it.

'It must have been a ghost, Nana,' I said.

Dara gulped, but I stared hard at him and

he never let on, which is pretty good for a baby like him.

'Yes,' said Nana. 'It must have been.'

'That's right,' said Uncle Dan, and he winked at me. 'Sure Dublin is an awful place for the ghosts.'

Even old Sinéad smiled at that.

5

Little Boy Lost

The next time we went to town, my ma wanted to go shopping, and she asked us if we'd be good while she tried on a few dresses. We said we would, but we soon got tired of being good.

'Race you up the escalator,' I said to Sinéad and Dara. 'That's a moving staircase,' I added, because I know there aren't any of those in Inishbeg.

'I know what an escalator is!' said Sinéad. 'I have been in a city before, you know.'

'Well, lah-di-dah,' I said. 'I was only trying to help.'

I won the escalator race because I'm used to dodging in and out between the people. Sinéad's too polite. She waits for people to move out of her way. Dara was too scared to even step on the escalator.

'Now for a real challenge!' I said. 'This time, I'll race you *down* the *up* escalator.'

'You can't go down the up escalator,' said Sinéad. 'Up escalators go up.'

'Ah, but *you* don't have to go up. Even if the escalator is going up, you can still go down, but you have to go very fast.'

'That sounds dangerous,' said Sinéad.

'It *is* dangerous,' I agreed. 'And it's against the rules.'

'We said we'd be good,' said Sinéad.

'We did,' I said. 'Are you chicken, so?'

'No,' said Sinéad, though I could see she didn't really like the idea.

So off we went. I won again. It paid old Sinéad back for winning that race in the country where I couldn't run properly because of wearing wellingtons.

Next thing, Sinéad looks around and says in a squeaky voice, 'Dara! Where's Dara?'

'Dunno,' I said, looking around.

'Oh, we've lost him! What if somebody's kidnapped him? What if he's wandered outside of the shop and gone out onto the street and been knocked over by a bus? What if he's met a *stranger*?'

She was nearly hysterical by now. I could see her point. He's a bit of a baby, Dara, but you'd be fond of him all the same. You wouldn't like to think of anything awful happening to him.

So I said, 'Let's go and look for him.'

'But where will we *start*?' wailed Sinéad.

Then I had one of my brilliant ideas.

'I know,' I said. 'We'll go to the Lost Property Office.'

'But Dara isn't property,' said Sinéad, hurrying after me.

'No, but he's lost. One out of two isn't bad.'

The people in the Lost Property Office hadn't got Dara, but they said we should go to the Information Desk, and so we set off there.

The woman at the Information Desk was very nice and helpful and she said she'd put a message out over the intercom, asking people if they saw Dara to send him to the Information Desk. She asked us for a description.

Sinéad was shaking all over. I think that's because she was worried about Dara being lost. I felt a bit sorry for her, so I thought I'd better do the talking.

'Small,' I said. 'Culchie.'

'I can't say that over the intercom,' the information woman said. '"Lost, one small culchie." You'll have to be more specific than that.'

'Bit of an eejit,' I said, helpfully.

'I beg your pardon,' says your one, getting all hoity-toity with me.

'No, no, not you, *him*,' I said.

'Oh,' she said. 'That's not much help. What was he wearing?'

'Clothes. Little boy clothes. I don't know, shorts and T-shirt, I think. Something bright.

Oh, I know, he has curly hair and he's five and a half.'

'That'll do,' said the woman, and next thing she starts talking into a microphone and her voice came out all over the shop, kind of boomy and whispery at the same time: 'Little boy lost. Little boy lost. A little boy of five and a half, with curly hair and wearing – eh – *bright* shorts and T-shirt is missing. If you find him, please bring him to the Information Desk on the ground floor.'

Sinéad started crying when she heard the voice, so the information woman came around to our side of the desk and got a chair for her and a glass of water.

Next thing, Ma appeared with her coat flying out behind her, galloping she was, across the floor of the shop. She was wearing a dress I'd never seen before.

'It's Dara!' she shouted. 'It's Dara who's

missing, isn't it? I knew it had to be when I heard the description. Oh my goodness!'

We're in for it now, I thought, losing Dara like that when we promised we'd be good. But luckily Ma decided it was all her fault. It never occurred to her that it was us that lost him.

'I shouldn't have left you on your own,' she said, and next thing, she starts crying too.

Just then the information woman came around to the front of the desk again and tried to move us to one side, as she couldn't have the desk all cluttered up with people crying.

'Excuse me,' she said to Ma, and next thing, she puts her hand down the back of Ma's coat. Ma got an awful shock and she snatched the woman's hand away.

'And what is this?' asked the woman, looking all smirky. She was holding a label in her hand, the kind they have on clothes in shops.

'It's a label,' I said.

'I know it's a label,' said Ms Information, 'and there are dressing rooms for trying things on. You can't go parading around the shop wearing our merchandise, especially not with your coat on over it. I'm afraid I am going to have to call Security.'

She was suddenly not as nice as she'd seemed at the start.

'But Dara is lost!'

I shouted at her.

'Oh my goodness!' said Ma again.

I didn't know whether she was still good-nessing about Dara or whether she was worried about Security being called.

'I can explain,' said Ma, when the security man came. He had a walkie-talkie and a nice face. 'I was trying on dresses, when I heard this message over the intercom about a little boy lost, and I knew it must be Dara, so I pan-icked. I pulled on my coat, forgetting that I was still wearing a dress I'd been trying on and I came racing here to see what was going on. Oh my goodness!'

'Well, well,' clucked the security man, tapping his chin with his walkie-talkie.

'You can't arrest her,' I said. 'We've lost Dara. We have to find Dara first. You can arrest her then if you like.'

'Michelle!' said Ma.

'I only meant …' I said. But then I stopped, before I made things even worse.

'I'm not going to arrest anyone,' said the security man. 'We have to find this child. Put out that message again, will you please, Ms Byrne? Thank you.'

'Little boy lost. Little boy lost. A little boy of five and a half, with curly hair, wearing shorts is missing. If you find him, please bring him to the Information Desk on the ground floor.'

We all waited for a while. Ma had stopped crying by now, but Sinéad was still snivelling a bit. Ma gave her a tissue.

At last the security man said we'd better go and look for him ourselves.

'What about the dress?' said Ms Byrne, but the security guard took no notice.

'I have a good idea where to try first,' he said to me. 'You'd be amazed the number of lost children who turn up in the toy department.'

So off we went, down two escalators to the toy department, Ma still wearing the shop's dress under her coat, and sure enough, there was Dara, drawing things on a blackboard. I can't imagine how he got there, considering

that he is afraid of escalators. There must be a
staircase, I suppose.

Ma gave a little gasp when she saw him and
she went running towards him, her coat flap-
ping again as she ran.

'Dara! Dara!' she called.

Sinéad ran after her, shouting, 'Dara!
Dara!' as well.

'I take it that's Dara,' said the security man
to me.

'That's him,' I said. 'He's a culchie.'

'Oh, well, that explains it,' said the security man. 'They can't cope with the city, you know, the culchies. Always getting lost.'

Then he winked. I liked him.

'Have a jelly baby,' he said, and he took a bag of them out of his pocket. I chose a purple one.

By now we'd caught up with Ma and Sinéad. They were both hugging Dara and kissing him, slobbering all over him. He didn't seem to mind.

'What were you doing, Dara?' asked Ma.

'I was drawing,' said Dara. 'I made a few cakes and things, in that kitchen over there, and I had a couple of wars with that fort, and I had a go on a trike, and then I thought I'd draw Mr Invisible.'

'You can't draw Mr Invisible,' I said.

'Well, you can draw his clothes,' said Dara. 'Only it's very hard to know where to put his hat when you can't see his head.'

'But Dara, Dara, did you not hear the announcement about the little boy that was lost?' asked Ma.

'Yeah, I did. Some Dublin lad, it must've been. *I* wouldn't get lost like that.'

'That was *you*, Dara,' said Ma.

'But I wasn't lost,' said Dara.

'Of course you were,' said Sinéad.

'No,' said Dara. 'I was here. I knew where I was. I wasn't lost.'

'But *we* didn't know where you were,' said Sinéad.

'Oh well, it must have been ye that were lost so,' said Dara.

'It doesn't matter now anyway,' said the security man. 'Nothing like a happy ending.'

'Thank you so much!' said Ma to the security man, and her eyes were shining. For one awful moment I thought she was going to kiss him, too, but she didn't.

'Have a jelly baby,' he said. 'And by the way, don't forget to go and change back out of that dress, or Ms Byrne will want me to arrest you.'

'Are you a guard?' asked Dara. 'Sort of,' said the security man.

Ma chose an orange jelly baby. She always does.

Sinéad said she wasn't allowed to take sweets from strangers and neither was Dara.

'Oh dear,' said Ma, with her orange jelly baby halfway to her mouth. 'That's right. I forgot.'

'But I'm not a stranger,' said the security man.

'And he's sort of a guard,' said Dara, very sensibly I have to say.

Sinéad still wasn't convinced.

'My name is Jim Reilly,' said the security

man, shaking hands with Sinéad. 'How do
you do, nice to meet you.' And then he shook
hands with all the rest of us, too. 'Now that
we've been introduced, have a jelly baby,
miss.'

Sinéad looked at Ma and Ma said it was OK,
so she chose a green one for herself and a
yellow one for Dara. *Exactly* what you'd
expect.

6

Dara and the Red Balloons

After we said goodbye to Jim Reilly, and Ma had changed back into her own clothes, we left the shop. Sinéad held Dara's hand all the time, in case he got lost on her again.

Ma said it was time to do something educational again, so we went to have a look at the Children of Lir. Not the real Children of Lir, because they've been dead for about fifty thousand million years and they'd be pretty smelly by now, the statue of them – half-swans, half-people. It always gives me the spooks.

'This isn't a proper garden,' Sinéad said when we got to the Garden of Remembrance, where the statue is. 'There's no grass.'

'There doesn't have to be grass,' I said. That's country people all over. Never happy unless there's green stuff everywhere. 'There's flowers.'

There were all these big RTÉ vans parked outside the Garden of Remembrance, and people were setting up cameras and lights and things. They were making some sort of a film.

'What's that big furry lollipop for?' Dara asked.

'It's a kind of microphone,' I explained. I know about these things because in the city, there's always people making films.

'Is that a swimming pool?' Dara asked then, looking into the big square pondy thing they have in the middle of the Garden of Remembrance.

'It's more a sort of a fountain,' I said.

'It doesn't look like a fountain,' said Sinéad, as if she was some sort of fountain expert as well as a garden expert. Them and their two bathrooms!

The people doing the filming started rushing around then and waving those clapper things they have and saying things like, 'Take Two'. It was very exciting. Ma made us all stand back so we didn't get into the movie by mistake. There were all these actor people wearing green leotards and floaty sort of dresses.

'They're always making films in Dublin,' I said to my cousins. 'You get tired of it, really.'

I don't think Sinéad believed me, but anyway she was too busy trying to wave at the camera behind Ma's back.

Then the person who seemed to be in charge, the director, I suppose, called out:

'Could we borrow a little boy for this scene? What about you?' and he was looking right at Dara.

'Me?' said Dara.

'Yes, would you like to be in the film? Where did you get those lovely curls?'

'I just grew them,' Dara said. 'I didn't get them anywhere.'

'Well, we need a little boy for this scene, and you look just right. Would your mammy mind if you sat there on the edge of the pond and looked into the water?'

'My mammy's in Inishbeg,' said Dara. 'Would I be a film star?'

'Definitely,' said the man, 'but I need a grown-up to say it's all right.'

'What kind of a film is it?' Ma asked.

'Oh, it's to promote tourism,' said the director, and he gave Ma his card, like they do in the films.

'It's all right so,' said my ma, 'as long as Dara doesn't mind. And make sure you don't topple in, Dara. We've had enough excitement for one day, I think.'

So Dara got to be in the movie. Can you believe it? He comes up here from the country for three days and suddenly he's on national television! But that's the thing about the city, you see, as I said to Sinéad. Anything can happen.

'Anything can happen in the country, too,' she said, tossing her head, but I know that's not true.

Dara didn't topple in, though he got his bottom wet because he got excited and splashed water all over the little wall thing he was sitting on, and then he sat in it, like the eejit that he is, but he didn't mind because he was going to be on the telly.

Afterwards we ran really fast down

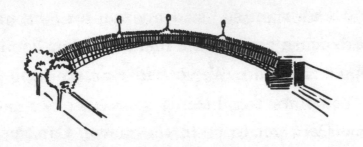

O'Connell Street and up the quays and along the boardwalk by the Ha'penny Bridge to help Dara's clothes to dry out.

'That's the Liffey,' I said, pointing into the river.

Dara looked into the river, all interested. I think maybe he was hoping someone would come along and admire his curls and ask if they could take a photo of him looking into the river.

We crossed the river then and went through Merchant's Arch to Temple Bar. It was thronged with people, as usual. Sinéad liked the funny chair with the leaves growing out of it, and Dara liked the cobblestones. We all got free balloons, big shiny red ones. Someone was giving them out for no reason, but I suppose it had to do with advertising something.

'You have to admit,' I said when we sat down on a bench to eat the ice-creams that Ma bought us, 'that the city is special.'

'How come?' said Sinéad.

'Well, people don't just walk up to you in the country and give you free balloons, now do they?'

'That's true,' said Sinéad. 'That has never happened in Inishbeg.'

'So you *see*,' I said, feeling very satisfied.

'Not really,' she said.

There's no convincing some people, is there?

'You'd want to lick down the side of your ice-cream cone,' Ma said to Dara. 'It's all melting.'

Dara stuck out his tongue and gave a big

slurp, but he was concentrating so hard on his ice-cream that he let go of his balloon, and it went sailing off.

Sinéad jumped up to try and catch it, and I jumped up too and we nearly got it, but it bobbed away from us and it went off up into the sky, way, way up over our heads and disappeared behind the clouds. One minute, there it was, all bright and red in the sky, and the next minute, it was gone.

Dara started to cry.

'Don't cry,' Sinéad said, but Dara went on crying.

'It would be better if you could cry quietly, Dara,' Ma said, 'because you're giving me an earache.'

That made Dara laugh, and then he started coughing, because if you cry and laugh at the same time, that's what happens. Sinéad

gave him her balloon then,
and I gave him mine as well,
and he stopped crying. We tied
the balloon strings to his wrists,
so they wouldn't float away, and I
told him he'd have to walk home
with big clumpy steps, or he might
go flying off in the air as well, with
the balloons.

He believed me! So off he goes,
clumping along down the quays,
with big monster steps, with his
knees sticking out one way and his
bum sticking out behind, concentrating on
not being airlifted out of it.

Sinéad and I were doubled up laughing at
him. He looked so funny, plodding along care-
fully, with a big wet patch still on his behind
where he sat on the wet wall by the pond and
ice-cream all over his face from licking his

cone. Everyone stopped to look at him and to have a giggle. I think they thought he was part of a street theatre act or something, with his red balloons and his funny walk and this concentrated look on his face.

'Has he got something wrong with his feet?' this woman asked Ma as we went past. 'You'd want to make sure his shoes fit. He looks as if he's in pain.'

'Ah no,' I said. 'It's only that he's a culchie. He's practising his clod-hopping.'

'Oh well, if that's all …' said the woman. 'Though mind you,' she said, and she gave me a big wink, 'I suppose that's bad enough.'

'There's nothing wrong with being a culchie,' Sinéad said to the woman.

Just then, this great big truck comes whooshing by, creating a big wind, and Dara's balloons started wobbling and bobbling like mad in the airstream.

'Oooh!' yelped Dara, sure he was going to be swooped up into the clouds at any minute, and he flung his two arms out and wrapped them around the woman's legs to anchor himself.

'Well, well,' said the woman. 'Culchies are very friendly, that's for sure. Going around hugging strangers on the street.'

Next time Sinéad and Dara come we are going to go to see a few more things, like the airport and the puppet theatre and the dead crusader in the crypt. Only we have to wait for Dara to grow up a bit first, because we don't want him getting lost again or losing his balloon or hugging people in the street, it's very embarrassing.

I hope he hurries up about it.